THIS BOOK BELONGS TO

children's choice®

For Laura and Gregory

The Monkey and the Crocodile

 A Children's Choice® Book Club Edition From Scholastic Book Services

The Monkey and the Crocodile

A JATAKA TALE FROM INDIA

Paul Galdone

Houghton Mifflin/Clarion Books/New York

Copyright © 1969 by Paul Galdone.
Book designed by Paul Galdone. Printed in the U.S.A.
ISBN 0-590-75932-9

Beside a river in the jungle stood a tall mango tree. In the tree lived many monkeys. They swung from branch to branch, eating fruit and chattering to each other.

Hungry crocodiles swam in the river and sunned themselves on the banks.

One young crocodile was hungrier than all the rest. He could never get enough to eat.

The young crocodile watched the monkeys for a long time. Then one day he said to a wise old crocodile: "I'd like to catch a monkey and eat him!"

"How would you ever catch a monkey?" asked the old crocodile. "You do not travel on land and monkeys do not go into the water. Besides, they are quicker than you are."

"They may be quicker," said the young crocodile, "but I am more cunning. You will see!"

For days the crocodile swam back and forth, studying the monkeys all the while.

Then he noticed one young monkey who was quicker than all the others. This monkey loved to jump to the highest branches of the tree and pick the ripe mangos at the very top.

"He's the one I want," the crocodile said to himself. "But how am I going to catch him?"

The crocodile thought and thought, and at last he had an idea.

"Monkey," he called, "wouldn't you like to come with me over to the island, where the fruit is so ripe?"

"Oh, yes," said the monkey. "But how can I go with you? I do not swim."

"I will take you on my back," said the crocodile, with a toothy smile.

The monkey was eager to get to the fruit, so he jumped down on the crocodile's back.

"Off we go!" said the crocodile, gliding through the water.

"This is a fine ride you are giving me," said the monkey.

"Do you think so? Well, how do you like this?" asked the crocodile. And suddenly he dived down into the water.

"Oh, please don't!" cried the monkey as he went under. He was afraid to let go and he did not know what to do.

When the crocodile came up, the monkey sputtered and choked. "Why did you take me under water, Crocodile?" he asked. "You know I can't swim!"

"Because I am going to drown you," replied the crocodile. "And then I am going to eat you."

The monkey shivered in fear. But he thought quickly and before the crocodile dived again, he said: "I wish you had told me you wanted to eat me. If I had known that, I would have brought my heart."

"Your heart?" asked the crocodile.

"Yes, it is the tastiest part of me. But I left it behind in the tree."

"Then we must go back and get it," said the crocodile, turning around.

"But we are so near the island," said the monkey. "Please take me there first."

"No," said the crocodile. "First I am taking you straight to your tree. You will get your heart and bring it to me at once. Then we will see about going to the island."

"Very well," said the monkey.

And the crocodile headed back to the river bank.

No sooner did the monkey jump onto the bank than up he swung into the tree. From the highest branch he called down to the crocodile: "My heart is way up here. If you want it, come for it! Come for it!" And he laughed and laughed while the crocodile thrashed his tail in anger.

That night the monkey moved far down river from the mango tree. He wanted to get away from the crocodile so he could live in peace.

But the crocodile was still determined to catch him. He searched and searched and finally he found the monkey, living in another tree.

Here a large rock rose out of the water, halfway between the monkey's new home and the island. The crocodile watched the monkey jumping from the river bank to the rock, and then to the island where the fruit trees were.

"Monkey will stay on the island all day," the crocodile thought to himself. "And I'll catch him on his way home tonight."

The monkey had a fine feast, while the crocodile swam about, watching him all day. Toward night, the crocodile crawled out of the water and lay on the rock, perfectly still.

When it grew dark among the trees, the monkey started for home. He ran down to the river bank, and there he stopped.

"What is the matter with the rock?" the monkey wondered. "I never saw it so high before. Something must be lying on it."

The monkey went to the water's edge and called: "Hello, Rock!"
No answer.
He called again: "Hello, Rock!"
Still no answer.

Three times the monkey called, and then he said: "Why is it, friend Rock, that you do not answer me tonight?"

"Oh," said the crocodile to himself, "the rock must talk to the monkey at night. I'll have to answer for the rock this time."

So he answered: "Yes, Monkey! What is it?"

The monkey laughed and said: "Oh, it's you, Crocodile, is it?"

"Yes," said the crocodile. "I am waiting here for you. And I am going to eat you up!"

"You have certainly caught me this time," said the monkey, sounding afraid. "There is no other way for me to go home. Open your mouth wide so I can jump right into it."

Now the monkey knew very well that when crocodiles open their mouths wide, they shut their eyes.

So while the crocodile lay on the rock with his mouth open and his eyes shut, the monkey jumped.

But not into his mouth!

He landed on the top of the crocodile's head, and then sprang quickly to the river bank.

Up he ran into his tree.

When the crocodile saw the trick the monkey had played on him, he said: "Monkey, I thought I was cunning, but you are much more cunning than I. And you know no fear. I will leave you alone after this."

"Thank you, Crocodile," said the monkey. "But I shall be on the watch for you just the same."

And so he was, and the crocodile never, never caught him.